P9-DEK-700

E
BAN

Banks, Kate,
1960-

Alphabet soup.

301721

DATE			

Discard
~~||||||||~~

BAKER & TAYLOR

ALPHABET SOUP

by Kate Banks

pictures by Peter Sís

DRAGONFLY BOOKS™ • ALFRED A. KNOPF • NEW YORK

DRAGONFLY BOOKS™ PUBLISHED BY ALFRED A. KNOPF, INC.

Text copyright © 1988 by Kate Banks
Illustrations copyright © 1988 by Peter Sís

All rights reserved under International and Pan-American
Copyright Conventions. Published in the United States of America
by Alfred A. Knopf, Inc., New York, and simultaneously in Canada
by Random House of Canada Limited, Toronto. Distributed
by Random House, Inc., New York. Originally published
in hardcover as a Borzoi Book by Alfred A. Knopf, Inc., in 1988.

Library of Congress Catalog Card Number: 87-3191
ISBN: 0-679-86723-6
First Dragonfly Books edition: September 1994

Manufactured in Singapore
10 9 8 7 6 5 4 3 2

301721

For Pierluigi
— K. B.

For my brother David
— P. S.

A boy did not want his lunch.
He squirmed.
He made faces.
"I won't eat it!" he shouted.
"My, you're as grumpy as a bear,"
said his mother.
The boy dipped his spoon into his soup
and growled.
"B-E-A-R," he said.

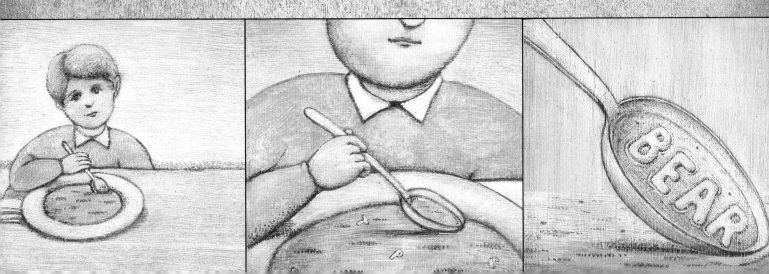

And there was a bear.
"Hello, Bear," said Boy.
"Hello, Boy," said Bear. "Come with me."
And off they went.

"Look!" said Bear.

An ogre stood in the road ahead of them.

"Who are you?" the ogre demanded.

"I am Boy and this is Bear," answered Boy.

"May we please pass?"

"No," said the ogre.

He would not let them by.

So Boy dipped his spoon into his soup.

"S-W-O-R-D," he said.

And there was a sword.
"On guard!" said Boy.
And he scared away the ogre.

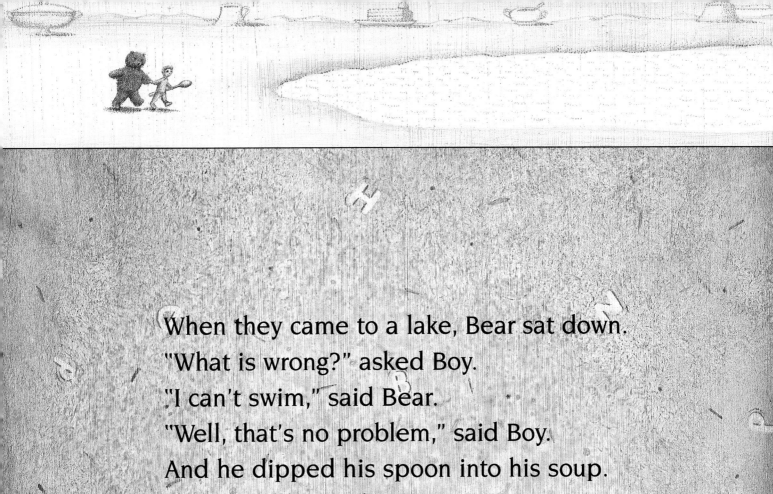

When they came to a lake, Bear sat down.
"What is wrong?" asked Boy.
"I can't swim," said Bear.
"Well, that's no problem," said Boy.
And he dipped his spoon into his soup.
"B-O-A-T," he said.

And there was a boat.
"All aboard!" said Boy.
And they climbed aboard.

Suddenly a large wave swept over the boat.
"Help!" cried Bear.
"I'll save you," said Boy.
And he dipped his spoon into his soup.
"N-E-T," he said.

And there was a net.
"You are heavy," said Boy
as he pulled Bear back into the boat.
And on they sailed.

"All ashore," said Boy
when they reached land.
"And up we go," said Bear.
They had come to a mountain.
"I can climb that," said Bear.
He tried once. He tried twice.
But Bear could not climb the mountain.
So Boy dipped his spoon into his soup.
"R-O-P-E," he said.

And there was a rope.
"Heave-ho," said Boy.
And Bear climbed up the mountain.

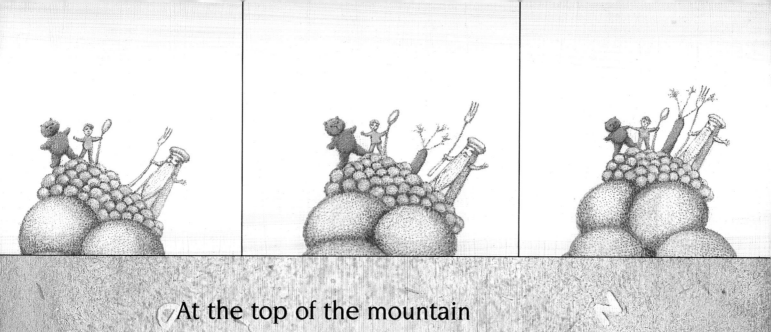

At the top of the mountain
they met a wizard.
"Welcome," he said.
He flashed his magic wand and turned
a little flower into a big tree.
Boy applauded.
"You are very clever," said Bear.
"But so is Boy."
Boy dipped his spoon into his soup.
"T-R-E-E," he said.

And there was a tree.
"You are more clever," said the wizard.
And he gave Boy his hat.

At the foot of the mountain
Boy and Bear met a crow.
"I'll take that hat," said the crow,
and he snatched it away from Boy.
"Give it back," said Boy.
The crow shook his head.
"You will be sorry," said Boy.
And he dipped his spoon into his soup.
"C-A-G-E," he said.

And there was a cage,
right around the crow.
Boy hung the cage from a branch.
"Serves him right," said Bear
as they marched on.

Night was falling
and the sky was growing dark.
"I hear thunder," said Bear.
A storm was coming. It began to rain.
"I am wet and cold," said Bear.
"Me, too," said Boy.
"Well?" said Bear, and he looked at Boy.
Boy dipped his spoon into his soup.
"H-O-U-S-E," he said.

And there was a house.
Boy knocked.
"Hello," said an old and little man.
"May we stay here for the night?"
asked Boy.
"I have only one bed,"
said the little man.
"But you may have it."
"Oh, no," said Boy,
and he dipped his spoon into his soup.
"B-E-D," he said.

And there was another bed – and another.
Now there was room for everyone.
In the morning Boy and Bear said good-bye.
"Come again," said the little man.

At last Boy and Bear came to a clearing.
The sun was shining.
"Let's rest," said Boy.
"All right," said Bear, "but I am hungry."
"Well," said Boy, "I can fix that."
And he handed Bear his bowl of soup.
Bear drank all of it.
"Hmmm…" he said, and he rubbed his belly.

"Hmmm..." said Boy, and he rubbed his belly.

Cherry Hill
Kindergarten
Center